For the children and staff of Coombe Bissett School—AM
For Carlos Campagnaro—SF

Snow leopards are beautiful animals that live on some of the highest mountains in the world.
They are perfectly adapted to their mountain home. They have big, fur-covered paws to keep them
safe on steep mountainsides, and long tails to keep their balance when chasing wild sheep and goats.
Those who share the land with snow leopards sometimes refer to them as "ghosts of the mountains"
because they are so well camouflaged that they are rarely seen.

Despite being well adapted to living in such rugged and remote habitats, snow leopards
are now endangered. There are only a few thousand left. Since 1981, the Snow Leopard Trust
has led efforts to ensure these beautiful cats continue to survive. They study the cats to learn more
about how much food and space they need. They also work with governments to help create or
expand protected areas. But parks and nature reserves are not enough: snow leopards need lots of space,
so the trust also works with communities that share the snow leopards' home so that both can live in peace.

To learn more about snow leopards and how you can help save them,
visit the Snow Leopard Trust at www.snowleopard.org.

THIS IS A BORZOI BOOK PUBLISHED BY ALFRED A. KNOPF

Text copyright © 2009 by Angela McAllister
Illustrations copyright © 2009 by Sarah Fox-Davies

All rights reserved. Published in the United States by Alfred A. Knopf, an imprint of
Random House Children's Books, a division of Random House, Inc., New York.
Originally published in paperback in Great Britain by Simon and Schuster Children's Publishing,
an imprint of Simon and Schuster UK Ltd., London, in 2009.

Knopf, Borzoi Books, and the colophon are registered trademarks of Random House, Inc.

Visit us on the Web! www.randomhouse.com/kids

Educators and librarians, for a variety of teaching tools, visit us at
www.randomhouse.com/teachers

Library of Congress Cataloging-in-Publication Data is available upon request.
ISBN 978-0-375-86788-0 (trade) — ISBN 978-0-375-96788-7 (lib. bdg.)

The text of this book is set in 18-point Berkeley Oldstyle.
The illustrations in this book were created using watercolor and pencil.

MANUFACTURED IN MALAYSIA
April 2011
10 9 8 7 6 5 4 3 2 1

First U.S. Edition

Little Mist

by Angela McAllister

Illustrated by Sarah Fox-Davies

ALFRED A. KNOPF

New York

Little Mist was born in a mountain cave.
Curled up in his mother's warmth, he
knew only her soft fur and sweet milk.

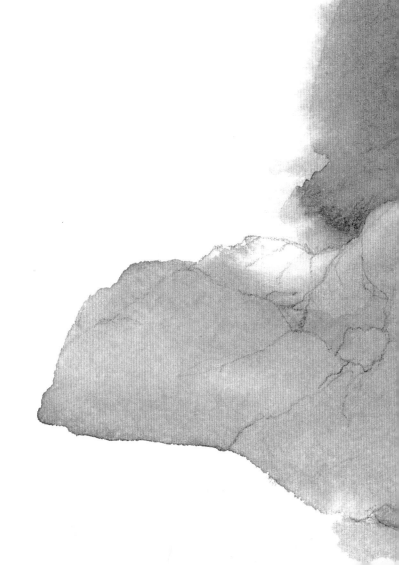

One day his mother opened her eyes and
stretched her paws.
"It is time, Little Mist," she said.
"Follow me."

She rose up, sniffed the air and padded out of the den.
Little Mist followed out of the dim hush. . .

. . . into bright, singing blue
and crisp, sparkling white.

"This is the world," said his mother.
"This is your world."

Little Mist rolled and tumbled in
the glistening snow.

He slipped and slid.

He pounced and shook his frosty fur.
"I like my world!" he laughed.

"There is more," said Little Mist's mother.

"The world stretches far and wide."

"More?" said Little Mist.

His mother rolled over and licked his eager face.

"Come, little one, come and see."

Little Mist saw the world stretching far and wide.

"Hear the river's voice," said his mother.

"Smell the pine trees. See the eagles soar.

Soon you'll chase butterflies in the cloud

forest and jump mountain streams."

"I like jumping!" said Little Mist.

His mother smiled.

"There is more. . . ."

She led him down, step by step,
to the water's edge.

Little Mist gazed at his reflection.
"The world looks so big," he said, "but I am only small."
His mother gently cuffed his nose.
"It is true. Just now you are a little heartbeat of the mountain,"
she said, "a tiny smudge in the snow."

"But one day you will be bigger than the red panda
that sleeps in the old oak tree. . . ."

"Stronger than the gray wolf leaping
from his rocky ledge. . . .

Faster than the moon bear watching
catfish at the waterfall. . . ."

"Sleeker than the shaggy yak that roams
across the grassland. . . .

Bolder than the musk deer that
slips through the pine forest. . . ."

"You will be more secret than the blue sheep
that grazes in the flower-filled meadow . . .

And as free as the wild wind that stirs the
glassy lake and dusts the high peak with snow."

"One day you will be a fine snow leopard, great hunter, King of the Mountains. But, until then, you are my own, my little cub."

Soon the setting sun began to dance on the mountaintop. Little Mist's mother led him back to the den.

She wrapped her soft, strong paws around him.

"Time to sleep," she purred.

But Little Mist was new and full of wonder.

He didn't want to sleep. He tiptoed to the mouth of the cave.

There he sat, wide-eyed beneath the stars, looking out at his world.

Little Mist couldn't wait to begin. . . .